MW00975441

This book was written for children everywhere.

There is not a dream that is too grand for you.
Dream big. Dream in color.
Never let your dream fade.

I thank my sister, Stacey, for her keen and helpful eye –
I enjoyed sharing the process with you.

Nicole, you're the best! Your help with the hard stuff is appreciated.

Finally, Jayce Alexander, I am so excited to see your face, to breathe in your scent, to hear your voice and soak in your laughter. I adore you already.

In honor of a special little guy, Hagan Hussey, 10% of every book sold will be donated to Cure Childhood Cancer in his name.

Hagan battled Posterior Fossa Ependymoma (brain cancer) for five of his eight years. He was a true Super Hero to so many.

If you would like to learn more about childhood cancer and donate, please visit **curechildhoodcancer.org**

Maybe

Written by Marcie Ostiguy
Illustrated by Maryna Kryvets

Maybe

Marcie@Ostiguy.net

Manufactured and Printed in China.
First edition
ISBN 978-1-7349852-0-7

Written by Marcie Ostiguy
Illustrated by Maryna Kryvets

Martha

Maybe one day,
I will wear a chef's hat.
I will make yummy food,
tasty treats,
and my guests will
always come back.

Maybe one day,
I will drive a yellow taxi.
I will drive people around exciting places,
calming countrysides and big,
flashy cities.

Maybe one day,
I will dance under bright lights.
I will stand on stage,
feeling so proud;
the applause at the end will be

thunderous
and
loud.

Maybe one day,
I will sit high on a shiny,
brown horse.
I will ride my horse through misty
meadows and across grainy sand,
all while wearing a cowgirl hat,
of course.

Maybe one day,
I will venture to the moon.
I will fly in a rocket ship,
and into space,
I will zoom!

PIZZA
Lieutenant Dave

Maybe one day,
I will drive a big,
red fire truck.
I will rush to help others,
making sure they feel safe.
I will always be there,
no matter the place.

Maybe one day,
I will fly a colorful kite for the whole day.
I will make it dance with the birds,
and in the wind, it will sway.

SIGNING

Maybe one day, I will write a book.
I will capture stories of adventures
that are kept safe in a nook.

Maybe one day,
I will be a mommy.
I will look at my children;
my heart will be full of love.
Hearing them laugh will be the most
beautiful song ever sung.

Maybe one day,
when I'm big and strong,
I will sit high up in a cloud
to watch the world
and protect it from
all that's wrong.

But for today, I will enjoy being me!